Usborne First Stories

GOLDILOCKS
AND THE
THREE BEARS

Retold by Heather Amery

Illustrated by Stephen Cartwright

Language Consultant: Betty Root
Reading and Language Information Centre
University of Reading, England

There is a little yellow duck to find on every page.

THE
THREE
BEARS

Once upon a time, there were three Bears who
lived in a cosy little cottage in the middle of a big
wood. There was great big Father Bear, there was
middle-sized Mother Bear and there was tiny wee
Baby Bear.

One morning, Mother Bear filled three bowls with porridge for the Bears' breakfast, but it was too hot to eat. "We'll go for a walk while it cools," said Father Bear, and the three Bears went out of the cottage and closed the door behind them.

Just then, along came a naughty little girl called
Goldilocks who was walking in the wood on her
own. Goldilocks peeped through the cottage
windows and when she saw there was no one at
home, she opened the door and looked in.

On the table were the bowls of porridge. First she tried Father Bear's porridge. "Too hot," she said.

Then she tried Mother Bear's porridge. "Too cold," she said. Then she tried Baby Bear's porridge. "Just right," she said, and she ate it all up.

Goldilocks was so full of porridge, she felt very sleepy. First she tried sitting in Father Bear's chair. "Too hard," she said.

Then she tried sitting in Mother Bear's chair. "Too soft," she said.

Then she tried sitting in Baby Bear's chair. "Just right," she said, and started to go to sleep. But, suddenly, there was a loud crack. Goldilocks screamed and tumbled on to the floor. She had broken Baby Bear's chair.

Goldilocks was cross. She got up and looked in the
bedroom. There were three beds. First she tried
lying on Father Bear's bed. "Too high," she said.

She climbed down and then tried lying on Mother
Bear's bed. "Too low," she said.

Then she tried lying on Baby Bear's bed. "Just right," she said. She pulled up the covers, snuggled down and was soon fast asleep. She did not hear the three Bears come back from the wood and into the cottage.

The Bears were hungry and wanted their breakfast.
Father Bear looked at his bowl. "Who's been eating
my porridge?" he said, in his great big voice. Mother
Bear looked at her bowl. "Who's been eating my
porridge?" she said, in her middle-sized voice.

Baby Bear sat at the table and looked at his empty bowl. "Who's been eating my porridge?" he said, in his tiny wee voice. "And they've eaten it all up." He began to cry. "Never mind," said Mother Bear, "I'll make some more."

Father Bear was very angry. "Someone has been in our cottage," he growled, and searched all round the room. Then he stopped and looked at his chair. "Who's been sitting in my chair?" he said, in his great big voice.

Mother Bear looked at her chair. "Who's been
sitting in my chair?" she said, in her middle-sized
voice. Baby Bear ran to his chair. "Who's been
sitting in my chair?" he said, in his tiny wee voice.
"And they've broken it all up."

The three Bears went into the bedroom. Father Bear looked at his bed. "Who's been sleeping in my bed?" he said, in his great big voice. Mother Bear looked at her bed. "Who's been sleeping in my bed?" she said, in her middle-sized voice.

Baby Bear ran to his bed. "Who's been sleeping in my bed?" he said, in his tiny wee voice, "And, look, she's still in it." Goldilocks woke up with a terrible fright and saw the three Bears standing round the bed, staring at her.

She screamed and jumped out of bed. She climbed
out of the window and ran home through the wood
to her mother as fast as she could. The three Bears
never, ever saw Goldilocks again and Goldilocks
never, ever went into the wood on her own again.

First published in 1987. Usborne Publishing Ltd, 83-85 Saffron Hill, London EC1N 8RT, England. © Usborne Publishing Ltd, 1987